WILLY THE SCRUB

BY JAMIE McEWAN

ILLUSTRATIONS BY VICTOR KENNEDY

DARBY CREEK PUBLISHING

To Robert Roger McEwan

Published by Darby Creek Publishing,
a division of Oxford Resources, Inc.
7858 Industrial Parkway
Plain City, OH 43064
www.darbycreekpublishing.com

Text copyright © 2004 by Jamie McEwan
Illustrations © 2004 by Darby Creek Publishing
Illustrations by Victor Kennedy
Design by Keith Van Norman

Cataloging-in-Publication Data

McEwan, James.
Willy the scrub / by Jamie McEwan.
         p. cm.
ISBN 1-58196-010-7
Summary: Willy and his friends have just started 5th grade and they want to be part of the "in" crowd, the jocks. The
fall football season leaves Willy a benchwarmer, or scrub, but he goes out for wrestling in the winter and things begin
to change.
1. Middle school students—Juvenile fiction. 2. Athletes—Juvenile fiction. 3. Wrestling—Juvenile fiction. 4.
Sportsmanship—Juvenile fiction. [1. Middle school students—Fiction. 2. Athletes—Fiction. 3. Wrestling—Fiction. 4.
Winning and losing—Fiction. 5. Sportsmanship—Fiction.] I. Title.
PZ7.M478463 Wi 2004
[Fic] dc22
OCLC: 52632857

Printed in the United States of America

First printing

2 4 6 8 10 9 7 5 3 1

CONTENTS

CHAPTER 1

DAY ONE

"It's Day One," said Willy. "A new year, a new school. We're fifth graders now. We're not in elementary school anymore. Everything's going to be different. *We're* going to be different."

"How?" his big friend Rufus asked. "How are we going to be different?"

Rufus gave a puzzled look around, as if he expected the difference to jump out at him from the hallway lockers. The four friends—Willy, Rufus, Dan, and Clara—were standing together on one side of their new school's big, wide hall. Crowds of kids they didn't know walked by.

"I'm saying it's time for a new start," said Willy. "A new me. I don't want to be just a face in the crowd. I want us to be part of the 'in' group. We can *be* the 'in' group. All of us from Davidson." Davidson was their old elementary school.

"I don't know," said Rufus.

"I do!" said Dan. "I like it! The new 'in'

group. That's us!" Dan was a little guy with hair that stuck straight up from his head. He could never stand still for long. Right now Dan was bouncing from one foot to the other, holding his hands up like a boxer. On one of his bounces, Dan bumped into a boy walking behind him.

"Hey, watch it, buddy," the other boy said without stopping.

"Who cares about being part of the 'in' group?" said Clara. "I know *I* don't."

"That's easy for you to say," said Willy. "You're probably the tallest person in the whole class. And you're a good athlete. You can afford to show up in pigtails like you were going into second grade instead of fifth."

"I'll take that as a compliment," said Clara, shaking her head so her pigtails swung back and forth, slapping against her face.

"The only problem is, most of the cool guys are jocks," said Willy.

"Yeah?" said Rufus. "Well, I was thinking of going out for football."

"Football! I've always wanted to play football," said Willy.

"Yeah!" shouted Dan. "We'll all go out for football. And we'll be cool! We'll be the best!"

"I don't know about that," said Rufus.

"You guys have never played football," said Clara. "Davidson Elementary never even had a team."

"I've played touch football plenty of times," said Dan.

"You should go out for soccer," said Clara. "Football's for dumb jocks."

"My father played football," said Willy.

"Um," said Clara. "Just kidding."

"Besides," said Willy, "we'll be happy to be *any* kind of jocks."

CHAPTER 2

GO, SCRUBS!

The next Monday Willy and Rufus and Dan showed up at the first practice in new football gear. It was a windy day. The football field was on the top of a hill. From there Willy could see the mountains all around. It was the right kind of day for an adventure. Willy was nervous, but he was excited, too.

"You guys are going out for football?" asked a kid named Biff. Biff was in the grade ahead of them, but he was no bigger than Willy. "I hope you're not a bunch of scrubs."

"What's a scrub?" asked Dan.

"A scrub is a lousy benchwarmer," said Biff. "Scrubs never get to play. And you look like scrubs to me."

"We'll scrub you, little man!" said Rufus.

But it turned out that Biff was a fast runner and a star player from last year. And Rufus was slow—much too slow to catch Biff.

At least Rufus was *big* and slow. Willy was small and slow. So was Dan.

"Come on, guys!" Coach Stone shouted at them during practice. "Use your ball skills! Use your quickness! Play hard!"

Willy used all the ball skills he had. He used all his quickness. He played as hard as he could.

Unfortunately, his "all" wasn't enough.

"What's the matter with you guys?" yelled the coach. "Biff ran right past you!"

"I told you," said Biff. "You guys are scrubs. Why don't you just quit?"

"He's right," said Rufus. "We should quit. I don't think we're cut out to be jocks."

"No!" said Dan. "We can't quit!"

"Why not?" asked Willy.

"Yeah, why not?" repeated Rufus.

"Because if we stick with it," said Dan, "and we work hard, at the end of the season, we'll win the big game and we'll be heroes. That's the way it works in the movies. Anything you can dream, you can do! Remember, a diamond is a lump of coal that stuck with it!"

"What?" asked Willy.

"A diamond is—oh, man," said Rufus. "You've been watching too many corny movies. What do you say, Willy? Do you want to quit?"

Willy thought about it. But it wasn't just that he wanted to be one of the "in" group.

He loved sports. He wanted to play football. Willy loved going to football games with his dad. He loved going to basketball games with his mom. And he loved playing every kind of sport in the yard with his little brother Joey. He wished he were a little better at playing sports. Maybe Dan was right. Maybe he would *get* better.

"No," said Willy. "This scrub will stick with it."

"Go, scrubs!" said Dan.

So they hung in through the whole season. They went to every practice. They tried hard. They stuck with it.

But they didn't turn into diamonds.

CHAPTER 3
GAME OVER

The whistle blew, ending the last football game of the season. Everybody on the team formed a line to slap hands with the other team.

Everybody except Willy.

Willy hadn't played. He hadn't played all season, and he hadn't played today. He had just sat on the bench, wearing a poncho to keep off the rain. So why should he slap hands?

"Hey, Willy, come on! You've got to get in line," said Rufus.

Willy got up slowly. "Okay, okay," he said.

"Good game, good game, good game," they all said, over and over, slapping hands. But it didn't mean anything. It was just what you had to say.

Willy's mom and dad came over to say "hi" after the game. Clara came over, too. All they could say was "hi." They couldn't say "congratulations" or "good game," because he hadn't played.

"Don't take it so hard," said Rufus as they walked back to the locker room.

"Yeah," said Dan. "So what if we lost? It really was a good game. It was close."

"I don't care that we lost," said Willy. "I just wanted to play."

"Yeah, me, too," said Dan. "Bummer." Dan looked sad. That wasn't like him.

"It's our first year," said Rufus, slapping them both on their shoulder pads. "We'll get better."

"It was your first year, too," said Willy. "You got to play."

"Only for one quarter," said Rufus.

"Maybe Dan and I are just too small for football," said Willy.

Biff heard them. "You're just as big as I am," said Biff, "and I played the whole game."

Biff was right. Biff was no bigger than Willy, but Biff was the first-string halfback. He had scored four touchdowns this season.

"It's not being small that makes you such losers," Biff went on. "It's just that you're lousy. You're pasty-faced nerds. You're benchwarmers. You're scrubs. You're slow, and you can't throw, and you can't catch. That's what makes you scrubs. And scrubs don't play."

"I know how to tackle!" yelled Dan. He jumped at Biff.

But Biff dodged him, and Dan fell down full-length in the mud. Biff was too fast for Dan.

Biff was too fast for any of them.

CHAPTER 4

A REAL JOCK

Willy stood in his living room. He looked at the pictures on the wall—pictures of Willy's father playing football and his mother playing basketball. They looked good. They looked like they were having a good time, too.

While Willy was still looking at the pictures, his father came in.

"I want to be an athlete like you, Dad," said Willy. "A real jock."

"A real jock?" repeated his father. "I'm not sure I ever was 'a real jock.' I was just an athlete. And you're an athlete, too. You just played a whole season of football."

"I just sat on the bench for a whole season of football," said Willy. "That's not playing. That doesn't make me an athlete. That just makes me a scrub."

"Didn't you play during practice?" asked his father.

"Sure. They needed two teams during

practice," said Willy, "so I played a lot then."

"So you played. That makes you an athlete. You don't have to win to be an athlete. You can be second-string and still be an athlete."

"I didn't like sitting on the bench through all the games," said Willy.

"I bet that was pretty frustrating," said his father. "But I'm glad you stayed on the team. It's good to be outside every day. And if you like to play and keep at it, you'll get better."

"Yeah, I guess I will. But I'll never be a real jock like Biff. Biff doesn't even have to try. He's just good. And the girls think he's so cool."

"Do you really want to be like Biff?"

"I don't know. Maybe, a little. Except a lot nicer."

His father laughed. "You don't have to be like Biff. I was never a natural like that. But I got by. Hey, help me make dinner, and we'll throw the ball around afterward."

"Sure," said Willy.

After dinner Willy and his father and mother and Joey all went into the backyard and played catch with Joey's little football. That was fun.

Willy came back into the house all hot

and sweaty. He went into his room and looked in the mirror.

He still didn't look like an athlete. He just looked like a pasty-faced nerd with red ears. He didn't *feel* like an athlete, either. No matter what his father said.

CHAPTER 5

GO WITH GROSS

"What sport are you going out for this winter?" Clara asked Willy at lunch the next day. "I'm going out for basketball," she went on. "That's the best. There's a girls' team here."

Last year Willy had played on the same basketball team as Clara. She was a better player than Willy. She was a lot taller, too.

"Maybe basketball," said Willy.

"I don't know," said Dan. "We're kind of short."

"Yeah," said Biff, walking behind them with his tray. "You're short, you can't jump, you can't handle the ball—you're a natural for basketball, Willy. Just like football. You'll be bad. And I don't mean *ba-ad*—I mean just plain old bad. Like lousy."

"Oh, beat it, Biff," said Clara. "Come back when you're not such an idiot. If ever."

Biff walked away, laughing.

"I'm going out for the wrestling team," said Rufus. "You ought to try it, guys. You might like wrestling."

"No way," said Willy. "That might be fine for a big guy like you. But I'm small. I'd get crushed in wrestling."

"No, you don't get it," said Rufus. "You only wrestle guys your own size. I'd wrestle big guys, and you'd wrestle small guys— guys in your own weight class."

"So what?" said Willy. "I still don't want to get body-slammed and kidney-punched and thrown through the ropes."

"No, no, you've been watching too much TV," said Rufus. "That stuff is faked. That's professional wrestling. That's not a sport. It's a show. It's made for TV. This is nothing like that. Nobody's allowed to slam or punch or anything."

"Are you sure?" asked Willy.

"They don't even have ropes," said Rufus.

"Yeah, wrestling," said Dan. "Sounds cool."

"Don't go out for wrestling!" said Clara. "It's disgusting. Sticking your head in some guy's armpit. It's gross!"

"I guess it is gross," said Rufus. "But gross isn't so bad, is it?"

"No," said Willy. "Gross is good. I can go with gross."

CHAPTER 6

GIVING UP

Wrestling was hard. Even worse, it turned out that Willy was in the same weight class as Biff.

Biff had wrestled last year. He knew what he was doing. Wrestling him was like wrestling an oily boa constrictor. Willy spent most of the time with his nose pushed into the mat. Then, every day, Biff turned Willy on his back and held his shoulders down for two seconds. That meant Willy was pinned. You got points for taking the other guy down or for escaping when he was in control. But it didn't matter how many points you had if you got pinned. If you got pinned, the match was over. You lost.

"I'm tired of wrestling you," Biff said to him at the end of the week. "You're not even good enough to give me a workout."

"Then you must be ready for me!" said Clint as he picked Biff up and tripped him to the mat.

Clint was the team captain. He was an

eighth grader. Willy had never noticed Clint before wrestling season. In school Clint was just a quiet kid who wore glasses and had long hair. Clint didn't look all that big or strong, but in about ten seconds, he had Biff pinned. Willy wished he could do that.

"I'm ready to quit," Rufus said to Willy later. "This isn't much fun. I ache all over." Rufus was a big guy, but he was slow. And he was not as strong as he looked. Guys a lot smaller than he was could beat him in practice.

"Yeah," said Willy. "My shoulders are killing me."

"No, we can't quit!" said Dan. "Pain is

just weakness leaving the body! What you can dream, you can do! Remember, a diamond is a lump of coal that—"

"Oh, come on," said Willy. "That's what you said about football! And you were wrong!"

"No, I wasn't wrong," said Dan. "It just takes a long time."

"We won't live long enough," said Rufus.

Clint let Biff go and walked over to them. "How's it going, guys?" Clint asked.

"I think Rufus and I are going to quit," said Willy.

"That would be too bad," said Clint. "You've already done the hardest part. You won't know whether it's going to pay off for a month or so. You should stick around to find out. It's kind of like an investment."

"An investment?" asked Willy.

"Yeah. You know? You pay now, and you win later," said Clint.

"And what if we lose later?" asked Rufus.

"That's a risk," said Clint. "But you guys are getting better all the time. Besides, Rufus, we need a heavyweight. There's nobody else in your weight class, so you'll be varsity. Won't that be cool?"

After Clint left, Willy said, "They need you, Rufus. But they don't need me. You should keep wrestling. I'll quit."

"Aw, man, it won't be as much fun without you," said Rufus.

"We'll miss you," said Dan.

"Yeah," said Willy, "but I won't miss being a scrub."

CHAPTER 7
NO FUN

On Monday afternoon Willy didn't go to wrestling practice. He hadn't told the coach he was quitting yet. He thought he'd tell him tomorrow.

Willy went home instead. He went to his room and played a computer game. In the game he could be big and strong. And he could win—most of the time.

But Willy knew that he was really only moving his fingers. The rest of his body wasn't doing anything. He wasn't being an athlete.

When he got tired of the game, he did some homework. Then Willy went into the living room and looked at the old pictures of his parents.

When Willy's little brother Joey got home from a friend's house, Willy and Joey wrestled on the carpet for a while. But it wasn't much fun wrestling with Joey. Joey was too small. It was too easy.

Willy was bored. It was no fun going to wrestling practice. But it was no fun not going, either.

After dinner Willy and Joey watched part of an action movie. The movie was exciting. But Willy knew he was just watching. Willy wasn't having an adventure. Somebody else was. Willy wanted to be the action hero himself.

The next afternoon Willy went back to wrestling practice.

"Good to see you, Willy," said Clint.

"Oh no," said Biff. "I was hoping we'd gotten rid of you for good."

"Thanks for coming back," said Rufus.

"We're going to have some fun, right?" said Dan.

"Fun, nothing," said Willy. "We're going to kick some butt! That's what we're going to do!"

CHAPTER 8

TOUGH SCRUBS

By Christmas vacation, Willy was still not kicking anybody's butt. In fact, Willy was still getting pinned every day. Every day he wondered why he hadn't quit. But every day he went back to the hot and smelly wrestling room with its padded walls.

He went back because he kept thinking

he might be learning something. He kept thinking he might be getting better. He kept thinking he might be able to beat Biff— someday.

At the end of the last practice before winter vacation, Clint got the whole team together. "Who's going to join me for workouts over Christmas break?" Clint asked. "You don't have to come. We can't have regular practices. And Coach is going to Florida. But if you want to get better, you've got to put in some extra work. Remember, when the going gets tough, the tough get going."

"Yeah, the tough get going straight to the

Bahamas," said Biff with a sneer. "Count me out. You wouldn't catch me dead around this place over vacation."

When they heard that, Willy and Dan and Rufus looked at each other. Then they all nodded. "Can the scrubs come?" asked Willy.

"Scrubs?" said Clint.

"That's what Biff calls us—the scrubs," said Rufus.

Clint laughed. "We'll all be scrubs then," said Clint. "It'll be the Scrubs' Special Holiday Workout."

The holiday workouts were hard. The guys wrestled. Then they climbed the rope.

Then they ran stairs. Then they did push-ups and sit-ups. Then they wrestled some more.

It was even harder than regular practices. And while they were sweating it out in the wrestling room, other kids were hanging out, taking it easy. But there was something cool about doing something that nobody else would do. It made them feel special.

"This is so much fun," said Willy at the end of one workout. "Aren't you glad you're not having a smoothie in the mall right now?"

At first the rest of them looked confused. Then Rufus said, "Yeah, or things could be even more horrible! We could be on the couch watching TV!"

"Or lying on the beach like Biff!" said Clint.

"Yeah, what a relief!" said Dan. "This is the life, man. Hey, let's do another set!"

They all laughed. Then they did two more sets.

CHAPTER 9
ONE POINT DOWN

When school started after vacation, Willy was doing better in practice. He didn't get so tired anymore. And he had learned some moves. He could score some points now, taking other kids down or reversing them. And he wasn't getting pinned. Much.

One afternoon the coach set up matches to decide who would wrestle varsity and who would wrestle J.V. Willy had to wrestle Biff. Willy was so nervous that when his turn came, he tripped over the edge of the mat. Biff didn't look nervous at all.

At first Biff was ahead. Then, in the middle of the match, Biff started to slow down. He was getting tired. Willy was tired, too, but he kept going hard. Willy started to score some points.

In the last period Biff was only one point ahead. Willy was on top, in control. Willy would have to turn Biff on his back to win. But Biff pulled in his arms and legs so Willy couldn't grab hold of them. Biff was hiding out like a turtle inside its shell.

"He's stalling!" Dan shouted. "Make him wrestle! Biff is stalling!"

When time ran out, Biff was still one point ahead. Biff won the match, so he would get to wrestle varsity.

"See?" said Biff, breathing hard. "You're still a scrub."

"What does that make you, Biff?" asked Rufus. "You were scared the whole last period. You had to stall or that scrub would have kicked your butt."

"It was so close," said Willy, shaking his head. "So close."

CHAPTER 10

WAY TO LOSE!

Biff wrestled varsity most of the season. Willy and Dan were on the J.V. squad. There weren't as many J.V. matches as varsity. Willy only wrestled twice, and he lost both times. But they were close matches.

One day Biff was telling the guys on the ice-hockey team how bad they were. "My grade-school team could have creamed you guys!" Biff told them. So they dared Biff to come to practice with them.

Biff borrowed skates and got out on the ice with the hockey team. But he wasn't used to skating. Biff slipped and hurt his knee. He showed up to school the next day on crutches.

Biff was on the injured list. Willy had to wrestle varsity for the last meet of the season. It was against their biggest rival, Central. Everybody came. Willy's mom and dad were there, and his little brother Joey. That wasn't surprising. But most of his class was there, too. Even Clara was there.

"Change your mind about wrestling being gross?" Willy asked her.

"No. I still think it's gross," said Clara. "But it's kind of cute-gross. Like a slobbery bulldog. You know what I mean?"

"Slobbery bulldog? I think I liked plain old gross better," said Willy.

"Good luck," said Clara. "Take it to him."

Knowing all these people were watching him made Willy nervous, especially when he found out he had to wrestle Central's captain, a kid named Bob Star.

"That guy pinned me last year," said Biff to Willy. "He hasn't lost a match all year.

He'll show you what a scrub you are."

Star had muscles popping out all over him. He had hair all over his forearms. He looked like he had to shave twice a day.

"Oh no," Willy said to Rufus. "What a monster! Why did I ever go out for this sport?"

"He's not going to kill you," said Rufus. "At least, I don't think he will."

"Great. Thanks for the encouragement," said Willy.

When Willy shook Star's hand, he saw that Star wasn't as big as he'd looked from across the mat. *Maybe*, thought Willy, *maybe I have a chance.*

The whistle blew. Star came charging out and took Willy down right away. He was quick.

Willy wrestled hard. He kept hoping that Star would get tired, but he didn't. Once Willy got rolled onto his back, but he got away before Star could pin him.

Then, in the last period, Star started to make mistakes. This was Willy's chance. Willy got control, and he turned Star over onto his back! People in the stands were screaming and jumping up and down.

"Pin to win!" the coach shouted. "Pin to win!"

But before Willy could hold down Star's

shoulders, the whistle blew. The match was over. Willy looked at the scoreboard. He had lost.

"Good match, buddy," said Star as they shook hands. Then the ref raised Star's hand in the air to show that Star was the winner.

Willy turned back to the team bench. To Willy's surprise the whole team and all the spectators stood up and cheered for him.

"Great effort," said the coach.

"See, you're not dead!" said Rufus.

"You lost, you scrub," said Biff.

"He did a lot better than you could have," Dan told Biff.

"Good match," everybody told him.

Clara patted him on the back.

His parents hugged him. "I told you, you don't have to win to be an athlete," said his father. "Way to be."

"I don't know what the big deal is," said Willy finally. "Biff's right, I lost."

"Yeah, but remember," said Clara, "it's not whether you win or lose that counts. It's how entertaining you are to watch!"

CHAPTER II

SCRUB CLUB

"So what's going to be your spring sport?" Rufus asked Dan and Willy the following week.

"Baseball, of course," said Willy.

"What else is there?" said Dan.

"Can you throw?" asked Clara.

"Sort of," said Willy.

"I bet you can't even throw from second to home," said Biff.

"Get out of here, Biff. Who asked you?" said Clara.

"I'm not going to do a school sport," said Rufus. "I'm joining this club that kayaks every day. Why don't you come and kayak with us?"

"Kayaking?" said Biff. "That's crazy. You wouldn't catch me dead doing that. Kayaking is weird. You're wet all the time. You wear this funny-looking gear. It's a sport for scrubs."

"For once I agree with Mr. Big Mouth," said Clara. "Kayaking *is* weird. It's all wet and gross."

"All the cool guys are playing lacrosse," said Biff.

"Let's see," said Willy. "It's crazy. It's wet. It's gross. It's for scrubs. Sounds like the perfect sport to me!"